the **BAD GUYS**

in

LOOK WHO'S TALKING

· AARON BLABEY ·

the BAD GUYS

in

SCHOLASTIC INC.

Go in peace . . .

IN LOVING
MEMORY

I mean . . .
have you seen *this*?

THE NEW
There's a New

Following the death of notorious crime figure Vinnie "The Big Bad" Wolf from a heart attack on Tuesday morning, rumors have been rife as to who would succeed him in taking over his wide-ranging underworld empire.

Sources can now confirm that the time for speculation is over; Moe Wolf, the only son of Vinnie (Vincent, 48 years) will run his father's operation from this point on. Little is known of the younger Wolf. It appears he is closely associated with a widely feared underworld figure referred to only as "Mr. Snake." He is allegedly also affiliated with two "fishy characters" whose identities are currently unconfirmed. "What can I tell you? He was born to be bad," commented one source who insisted on remaining anonymous for fear of retribution from Wolf and his crew.

S BULLETIN
Beast in Town

FROM BAD TO WORSE? *Moe Wolf (pictured left) has inherited a legacy of fear and intimidation. Will our city ever be safe? Or is this the beginning of a new wave of crime?*

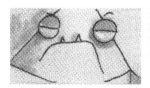 

SLEEP WITH THE FISHES? *Are these the new faces of fear in our community? If you have any information regarding the identity of these two shady characters, please call 1-800-BAD-FISH.*

Pet store owner Mr. Ho h this to say — "The snake ju went crazy. He ate everythin in the store and then tried to me!" Obviously, with frien like this, the young Wolf is onl hardening his already terrify reputation.

I'm the new

BIG BAD WOLF!

· CHAPTER 1 ·
WHAT DID

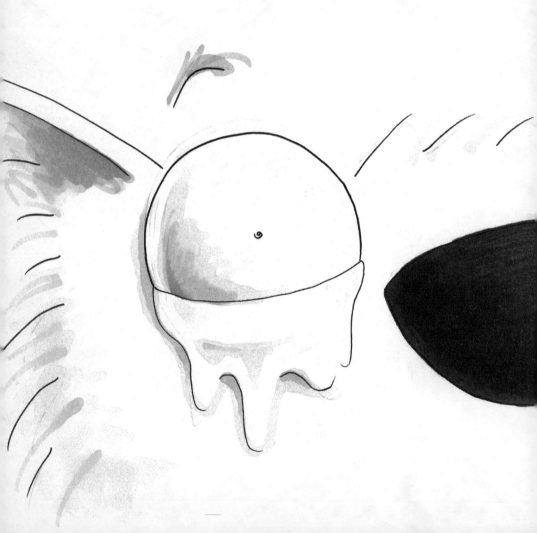

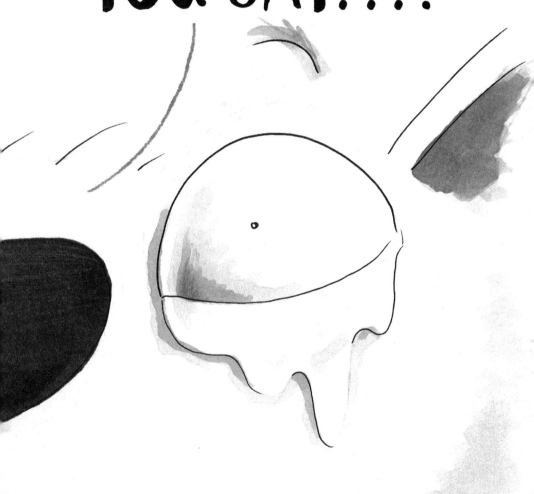

You can *talk*?

Not here.
We need to leave.
Right now.

We can't leave her.

We can't just
leave her.

Ellen sacrificed
everything for me.
We have to keep going.
We owe it to her.

Come with me.

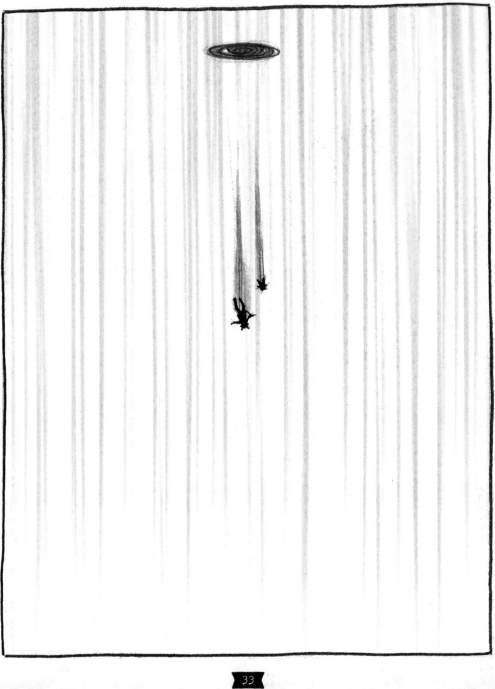

· CHAPTER 2 ·
RHONDA

FOOMP!

SMACK!

I thought you'd
have gotten the
hang of that
by now . . .

Wha . . .

This way.

They won't be far behind.
We need to get moving.

What's up?

Pffff . . .

OK.
We don't have long . . .
but I imagine you probably have

A FEW QUESTIONS.

What do you want to know?

AW WRIGHT! GIMME A BREAK HERE.

Just breathe.

AW WRIGHT. WHOOOO ARE YOOOOU?!

Who am I?
YESYESYES,
WHOOOOOARE
YOOOOOOU?!
Breeeeathe . . .
GLARGLE
AARGH
BLARRGL–
BLAAR!

I am *Rhonda.*

AND?!

And I'm probably
A LITTLE OLDER
than you might imagine . . .

You see, that centipede
has been the

ULTIMATE FORCE
OF DARKNESS

in the multiverse

since the

BEGINNING
OF TIME.

Trillions of years, in fact.

But, thankfully,
there is no dark without light.

I am the light.

That's me.

So, *what* are you saying?
You're the
ULTIMATE FORCE OF GOODNESS?

Yes.
That is what I'm saying.

For many lifetimes
I have been able to protect the
multiverse because I've had an

ADVANTAGE
over Splaarghön—

I CAN GLIDE THROUGH
SPACE AND TIME.

DISTANCE
is no obstacle for me.

TIME is no obstacle.

I can

CROSS GALAXIES . . .

I can

VISIT THE FUTURE . . .

I can

VISIT THE PAST . . .

I have **NO LIMITATIONS.**

BUT . . .

Over time, Splaarghön began to develop the
SAME POWERS.
He found my wormholes
and loopholes and learned to
MANIPULATE OTHERS
to find my **DOORWAYS . . .**

The DOORWAYS are

YOURS?!

Yes, and he was never meant
to know about them . . .

But he found out and
used all his power to

OPEN THEM.

That said, for a trillion years I kept him at bay.

Well, I did until . . .

THE PROPHECY.

The *prophecy*?!
What prophecy?!

BUT . . .

I also saw a VISION of a
CREATURE
who would allow
Splaarghön to enter the
FINAL REALM
and
TAKE CONTROL
of the
**ENTIRE
MULTIVERSE.**

A *creature?*
You don't mean . . .

The Vision was of
A SERPENT.
The Vision was of a . . .

. . . snake.

· CHAPTER 3 ·
IF YOUR LIFE WAS A SERIES

We should walk and talk.
They'll be coming.

Wait up!
So you're telling me
that after TRILLIONS
of years protecting the
multiverse, you

SUDDENLY

knew that disaster was
coming because you had
a VISION of . . .

. . . my little buddy *Snake*?!

Yes.

But he was just a
SMALL-TIME CROOK!
A small-time crook who was
trying to be **GOOD,** I might add.
Out of all the snakes in the world,
how on Earth did you know it was him?!

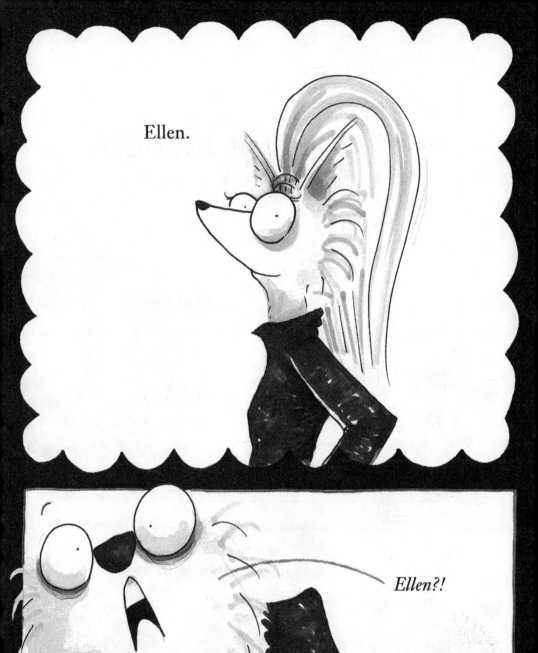

OK.
Let's imagine that your life is a
BOOK SERIES.
Can you do that?

Yes.
Yes, I can,
as a matter of fact . . .

Well, then, cast your
mind back to . . .

BOOK THREE!

Do you remember that?
When you thought you met a **NINJA**
who turned out to be **ELLEN?**

But she was there that day
because she was following
MARMALADE...

No.
She knew Marmalade was a rotten
little egg, but she also knew he wasn't the
REAL THREAT.

She was *mostly* there to get close
to Snake and keep an eye out
for any signs of . . . trouble.
And when trouble came,
IF your life was a series,
it would have been in . . .

BOOK ELEVEN!

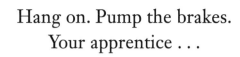

Hang on. Pump the brakes.
Your apprentice . . .
Ellen isn't trillions of years old, too, is she?!

No, no . . .
she's mortal.
Like you.
But she *is* rather exceptional.

I noticed.

She was **ORPHANED** when she was young . . .

I found her wandering alone as a child.

There was something
EXTRAORDINARY
about her, even then.

It wasn't always easy . . .

. . . but her heart was always pure.
I don't know why, but after so many
millions of years, I decided to

TRAIN SOMEONE
and
SHARE MY SECRETS.

She did.

She did that for *me*.

She volunteered to be
A DECOY.
She sacrificed herself by diverting the
attention of all evil toward *her*.

She was a decoy?
But her

POWERS!

She had amazing powers!

When Splaarghön burst
through into our realm, I

TRANSFERRED

some of my power.

WHEN?!

If your life was a series, it would have been in

BOOK ELEVEN.

Probably on

PAGE 144 . . .

if I had to guess and be really specific for some reason . . .

Here I am, transferring my power . . .

I *remember* that!

Wait!
You gave Ellen powers . . . but you gave powers to

PIRANHA,

too?!

Yes. I thought it would be safer if there was someone else I could **SECRETLY SEND MESSAGES TO.** That way I could send guidance to either of them if we all got split up.

He's done a rather marvelous job, too, whether he knows it or not. But there was also one completely **UNEXPECTED SIDE EFFECT . . .**

Piranha accidentally passed some of my power onto his **FATHER.**

This proved wonderfully useful, though, as it allowed *them* to **COMMUNICATE,** too.

PAPA!

PEPE?!

And it also helped me
in other ways . . .

GLARHGLE!

So Ellen doesn't really have
MAGIC HANDS?

No.
But I'll tell you this—
if any of you tried to do what she
just did, my power would have

DESTROYED YOU.

She spent her whole life training
for what she just did. Only someone as

AMAZING

as her could have pulled it off.

She sacrificed herself for all of us.

She is a true *hero*.

· CHAPTER 4 ·
IT REALLY IS KINDA LIKE A SERIES

We might want to try jogging, OK?

So **THE OTHERS** were never actually meant to join with Ellen?

No.
They were always coming for me.
Ellen just tricked the forces of darkness into *thinking* they were coming for her.
Tricky fox.

So . . .

. . . they're *part of you* now?

Yes.
They **ARE** me.

I hid parts of myself when
I knew Splaarghön was
coming to destroy me.
I hid everything but my

PUREST SURVIVAL
INSTINCTS . . .

That made me a little . . .
GROUCHY.
Ellen even started calling me
SHORTFUSE.

Cheeky fox.

I hid my
TENACITY...

I hid my
INTEGRITY...

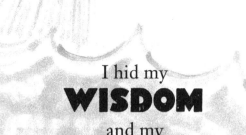

I hid my
WISDOM
and my
MAGICAL HAIR...

MILTON?!

Yes.

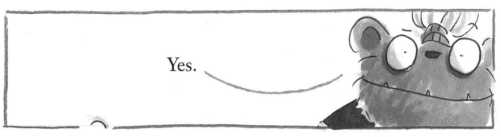

But HOW?!

Remember when you went into **SPACE** in that **STOLEN ROCKET?**

Do you mean . . .

Well, what you don't know is that I came along on that trip to keep an eye on you. There I am up top, next to the arrow. See?

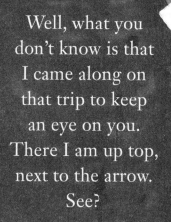

And I must confess, I tinkered with the
ESCAPE PODS
so that when you took off . . .

It was **DELIBERATE?!**

Yes.

So, if our life was a series, then that *dinosaur episode* actually wasn't totally random? Because, if our life was a series, that book would *probably* have made some of the more critical readers say, "Oh, this book is a bit far-fetched and pointless. This series has completely derailed." Are you telling me they would be

WRONG?!

Yes. They would be
COMPLETELY WRONG.

If your life was a series, all your readers would be rewarded by discovering that

NOTHING IS RANDOM.

In fact, any negative critics would find themselves completely agog and with *egg on their faces*. They'd probably even rethink some of their *life choices* and become *kinder in general*.

So, you sent us back to get Milton because he was *part of you* that you'd hidden **60 MILLION YEARS IN THE PAST?**

Yes.
But I made a **TERRIBLE MISTAKE.**

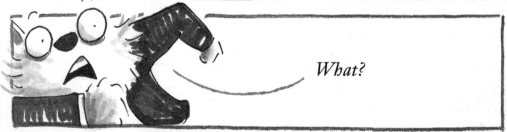

What?

Do you remember how the ESCAPE POD gave you **SUPERPOWERS?**

Yes! The end of **BOOK SEVEN,** and then expanded upon brilliantly in **BOOK EIGHT!**

Well, that was a SIDE EFFECT
of my powers. I didn't think it would hurt.

But . . . when
ALL THAT POWER
got diverted solely into Snake . . .

The climax of
BOOK NINE
and the surprise reveal in the
dynamic story arc finale in
BOOK TEN?!

Yes.
And THAT started his
descent into darkness.

I undid all the good work
you had done.

You were right. Your *instinct* was right.
Snake is good at heart.

But so many things have
pulled him in the
**WRONG
DIRECTION.**

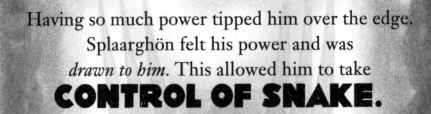

Having so much power tipped him over the edge.
Splaarghön felt his power and was
drawn to him. This allowed him to take

CONTROL OF SNAKE.

And *this* caused the
prophecy to come true.

After protecting the multiverse for so long . . .

I am the one who has put it in danger.

But now you're **COMPLETE** again. You are back with The Others.

Doesn't that mean you're ready to defeat him?

I wish it was that simple.

The prophecy spoke of a great battle between me and Splaarghön, yes . . .

But it also foretold of ANOTHER battle, to be fought at the same time, between **THE SERPENT** and **THE BEAST.**

The beast?!
What beast?

The beast,
I'm afraid, is . . .

• CHAPTER 5 •
THE BEAST

Mr. Wolf, I've been watching you . . .

. . . for a **VERY** long time . . .

I'd monitored many snakes and many beasts for thousands of years . . .

But the day I saw this . . .

I had a very particular
feeling of dread.

Why?

Because you two just seemed
like the perfect suspects.

Story of my life . . .

Yes, I apologize.
But please know how much
I respect what you've done.
How MUCH you have changed!

Ellen was
so inspired
by you, too.

You are extraordinary, Mr. Wolf.
You may be THE BEAST.
But you are a beast on the
SIDE OF GOOD.

And you have
nothing less than the
**FATE OF THE
MULTIVERSE**
in your paws.

LEAVE ME?!

HERE?!

Why?!

I must take my
TRUE FORM.
And that will take me a little while.

Your true form?
What . . . you don't
really look like a . . .

*What sort of animal
are you exactly?*

If your life was a series,
you wouldn't be the first to
ask that question.

 I'm disguised as a
TASMANIAN DEVIL.
Obviously.

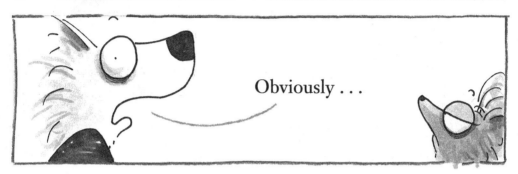 Obviously . . .

But now I must
SHED MY DISGUISE.

It was a pretty good one, too.
Did you notice how **ABE**
didn't even recognize me?
I was quite pleased with that!

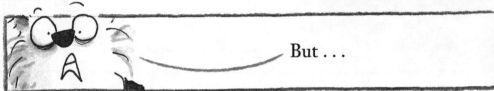

But . . .

STAY STRONG,
Mr. Wolf.
I shall return.

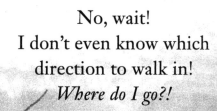

No, wait!
I don't even know which
direction to walk in!
Where do I go?!

You must head directly
toward Splaarghön.
And he's easy to find . . .

You just walk in whichever
direction feels the most . . .

. . . bad.

But . . .

· CHAPTER 6 ·
THE NIGHTMARE REALM

Great.

What are you doing here, Wolf?

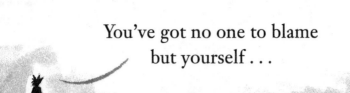

You've got no one to blame
but yourself . . .

"Hey, guys! Let's go good!
Let's be the Good Guys Club!"

You idiot.

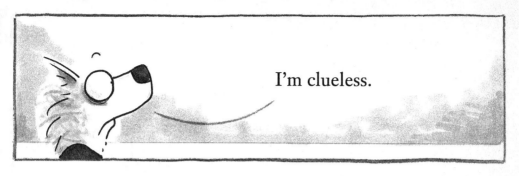

I'm clueless.

I literally have no clues.

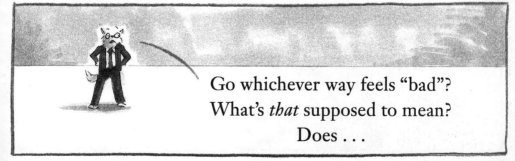

Go whichever way feels "bad"?
What's *that* supposed to mean?
Does . . .

OK.

No more skipping . . .

Sure, look, that was **WEIRD.**
Maybe I'm just *tired*.

Tired and *seeing things* . . .

FOOF!

OOOOOOOOO...

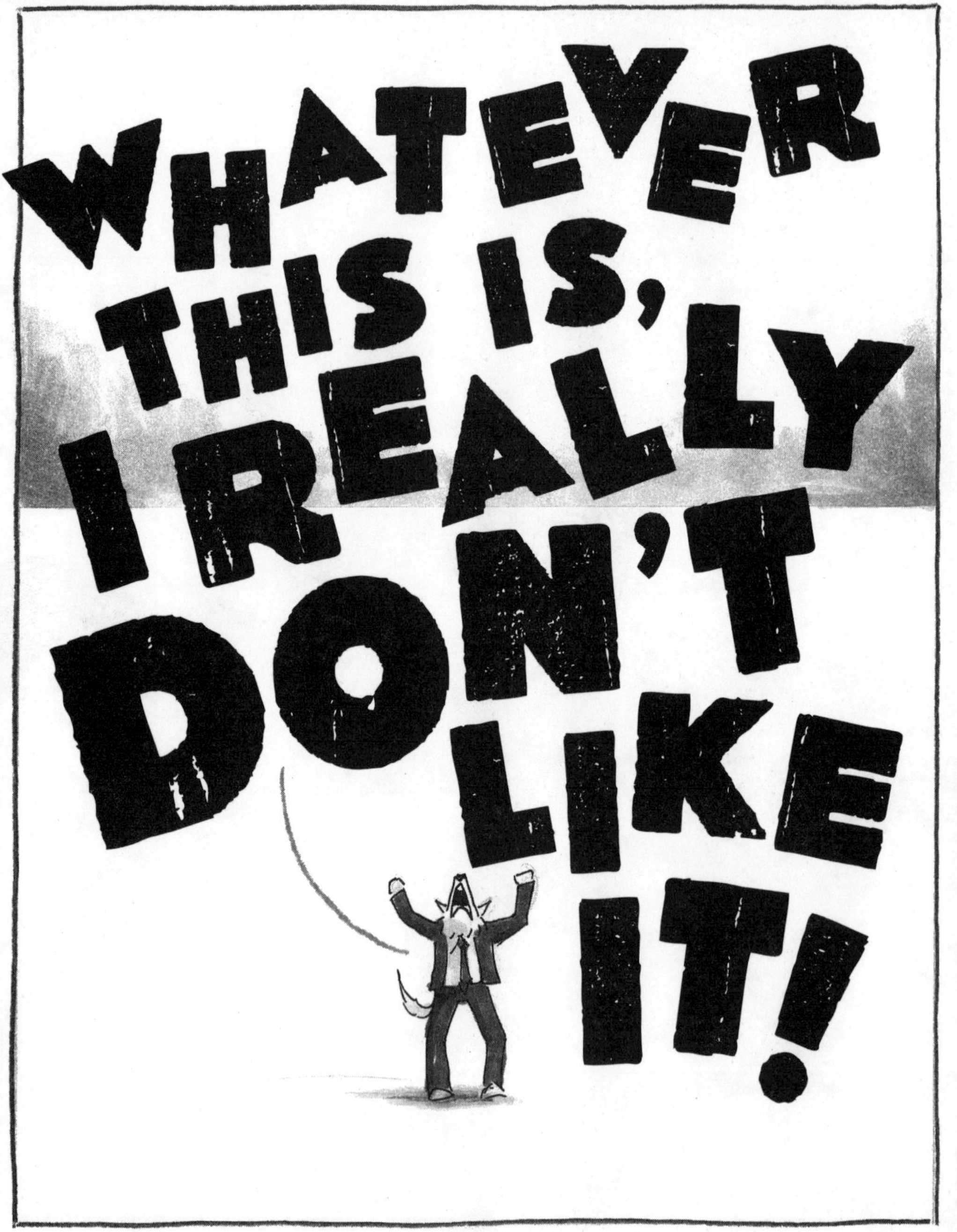
WHATEVER THIS IS, I REALLY DON'T LIKE IT!

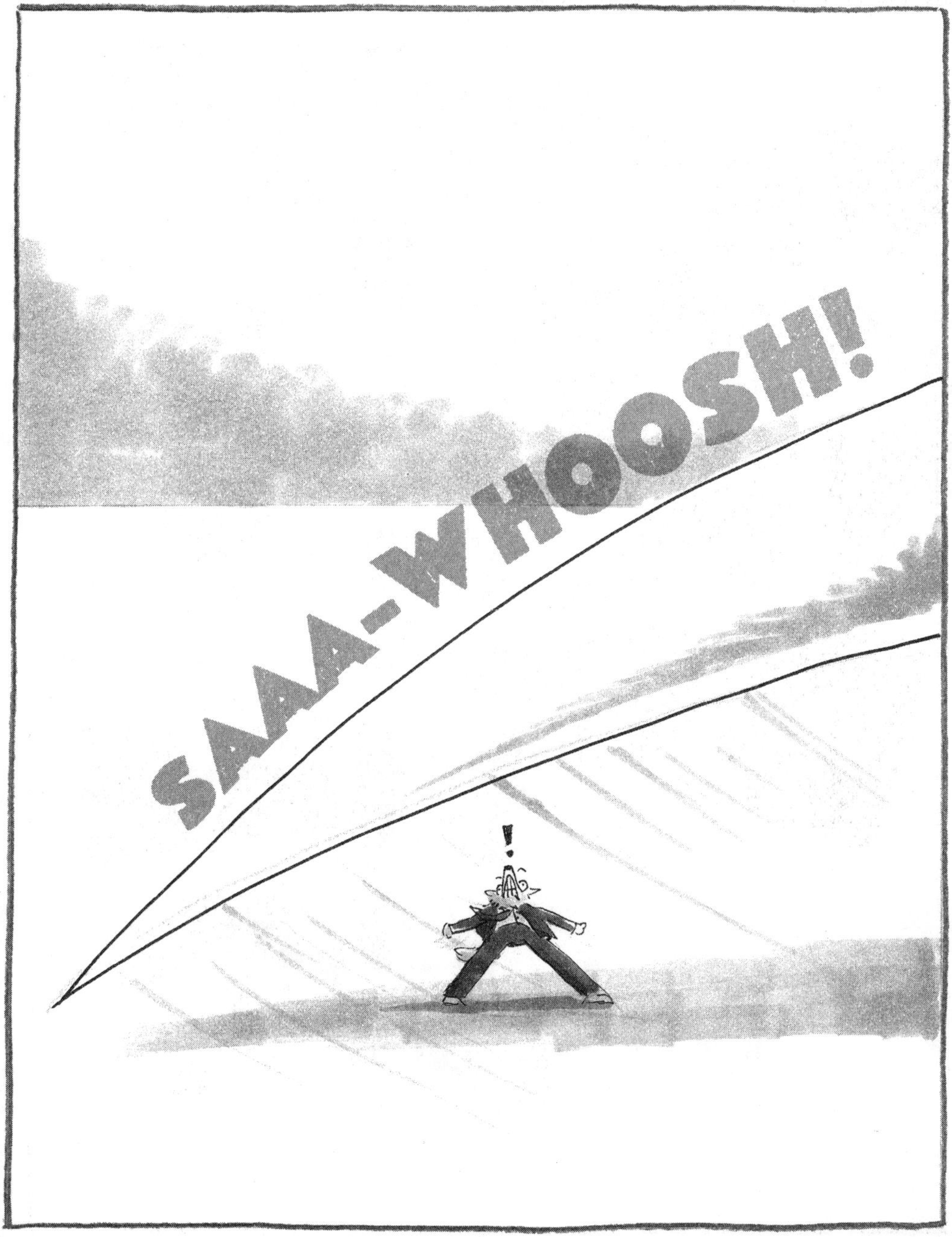
SAAA-WHOOSH!
!

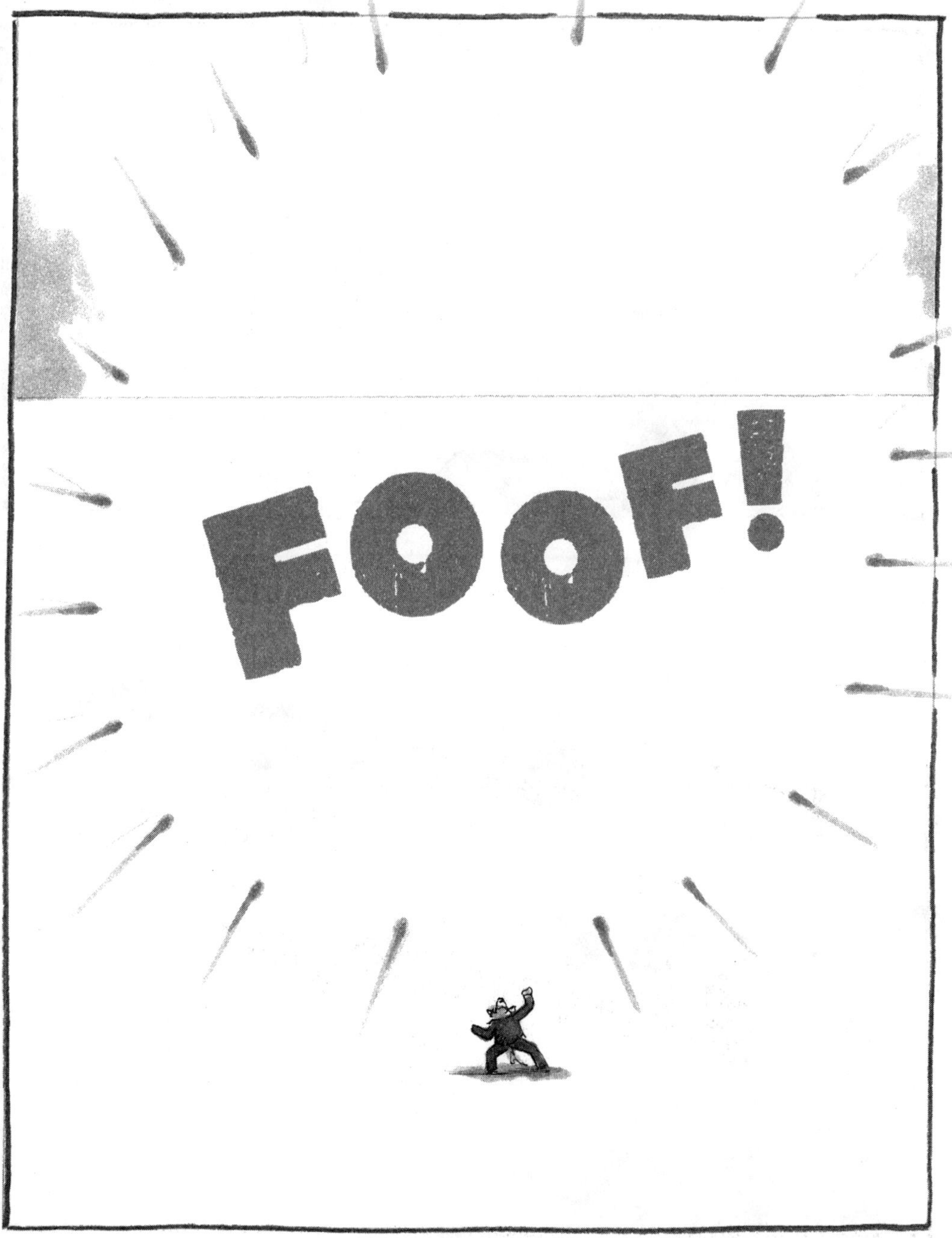
FOOF!

· CHAPTER 7 ·
OLD PALS

That was what awaits you
if you stay on this path.

Listen to me, buddy . . .

I *know stuff* now.

I know the truth about the centipede

and I know the truth about . . . The One . . .

and I **KNOW** that you're on

THE WRONG TEAM, man.

This is going to end **BADLY.**

Nothing.
It reminds me of nothing.

Oh, you can do better than that.
What does it remind you of?

It reminds me of a
NIGHTMARE.

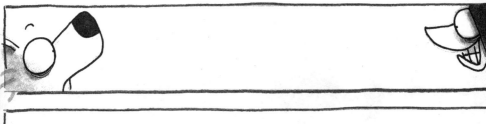

Don't you see?!

This is precisely where we DO belong!
This is the

NIGHTMARE REALM!

This is where the stuff of
NIGHTMARES was BORN!

That's crazy!
I wasn't born here
and neither
were you.

Perhaps not *literally* . . .

BUT the **IDEA** of us was born here!

THE MYTHOLOGY OF MONSTERS!

The
CREATURE UNDER THE BED!

The
SCARY
ones who hold so much power over the SCARED ones.

WE ARE
POWERFUL
HERE!

And when we HARNESS that power, we can take it out into the multiverse and have

ANYTHING WE WANT!

It's

BEAUTIFUL,

Wolf.

And it's time.

You've run out of chances, pal.

Are you ready to stop being stubborn and just be what you were **BORN TO BE?**

REMEMBER...

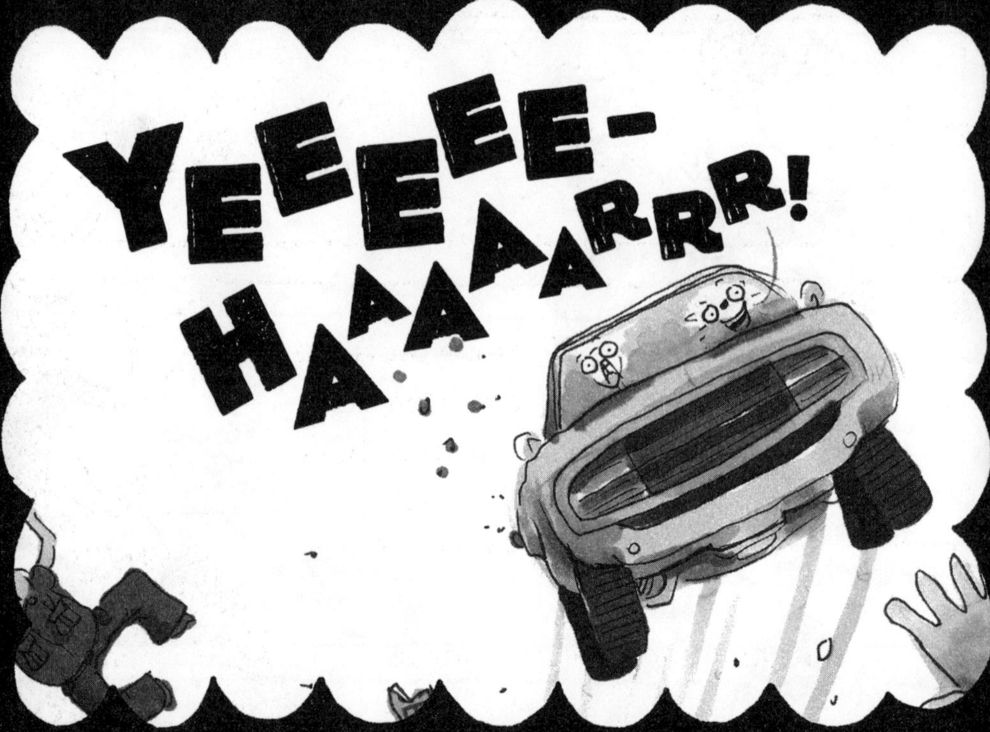
YEEEEE-HAAAAARRR!

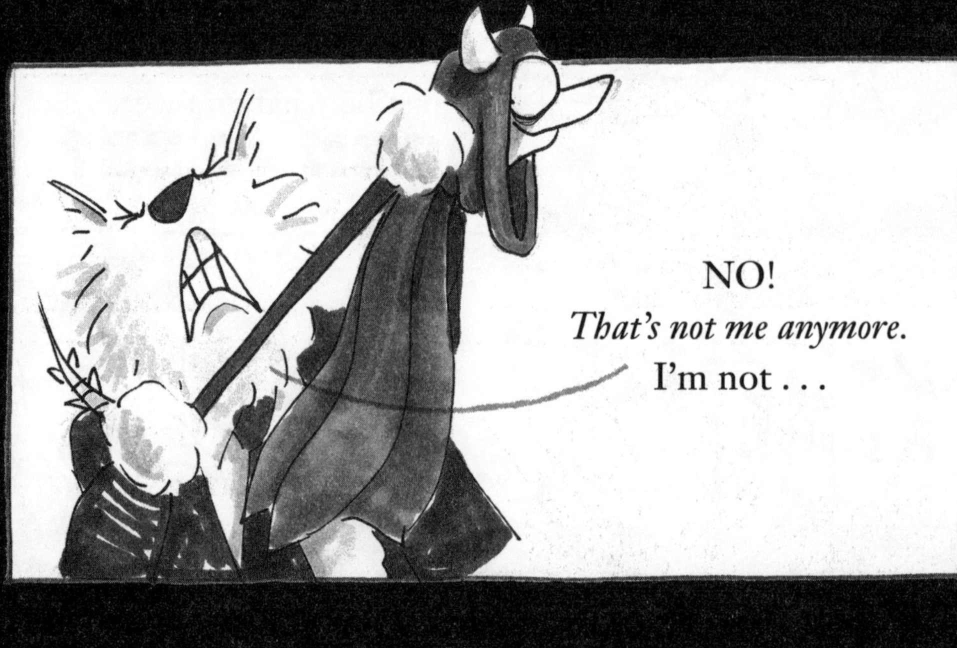
NO!
That's not me anymore.
I'm not . . .

Not what?
Not **BAD?**

I think you've just forgotten how good it feels, buddy.

But don't take *my* word for it.

HEY, YOU!

How does it feel to be BAD?!

It feels

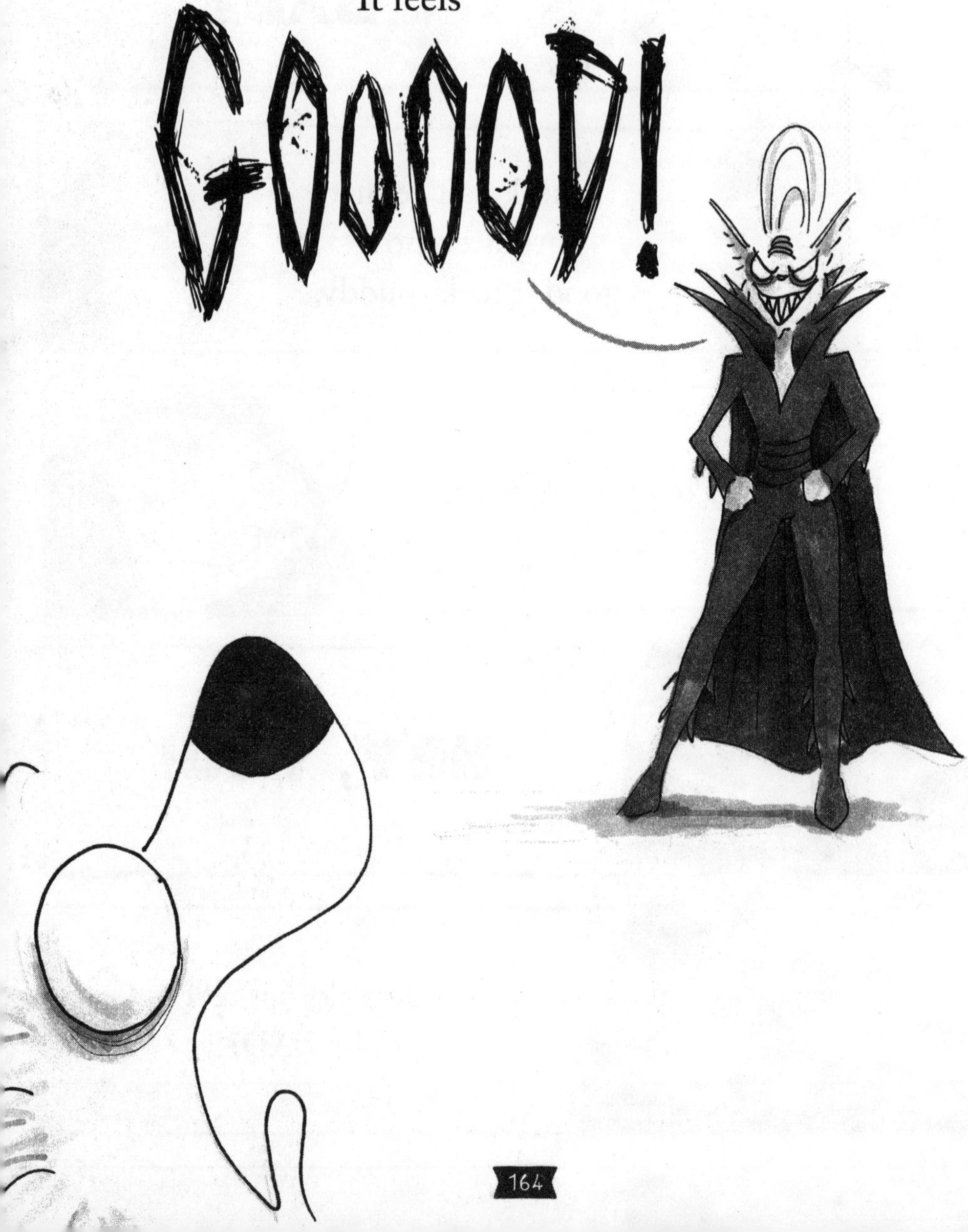

· CHAPTER 8 ·
TRICKY FOX

No . . .

Don't be afraid, Wolfie.

You don't know
what you're missing!

Ellen . . .
not you . . .

OH,
DON'T BE
SUCH A
BABY!

THIS ISN'T
EITHER OF YOU . . .

But it IS us . . .

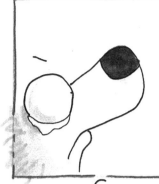

AND WE'VE NEVER BEEN **HAPPIER**...

No ...

IT'S NOT YOU!

IT'S *SPLAARG* . . .

· CHAPTER 9 ·
THE DREAD OVERLORD

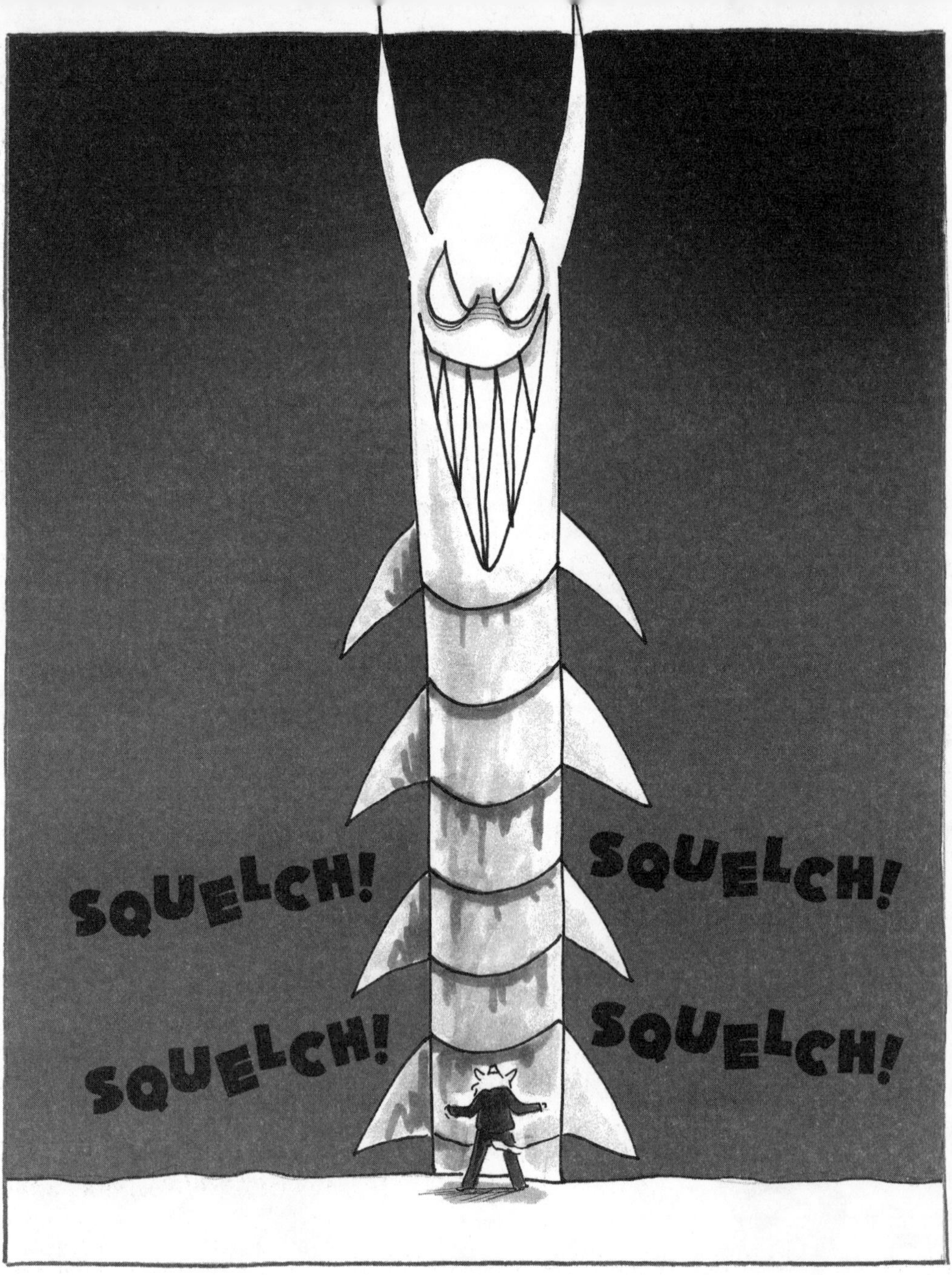
SQUELCH!
SQUELCH!
SQUELCH!
SQUELCH!

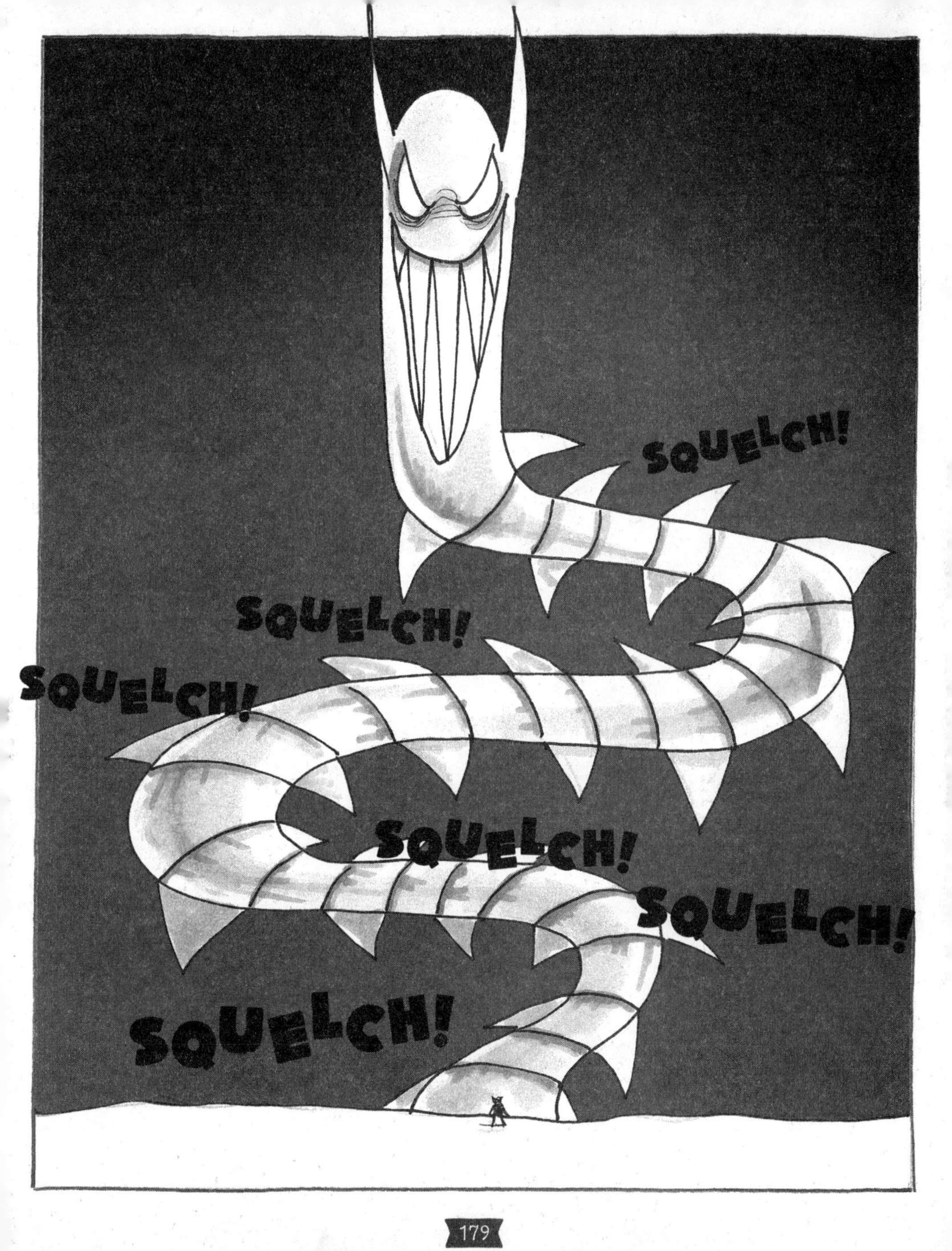
SQUELCH!
SQUELCH!
SQUELCH!
SQUELCH!
SQUELCH!
SQUELCH!

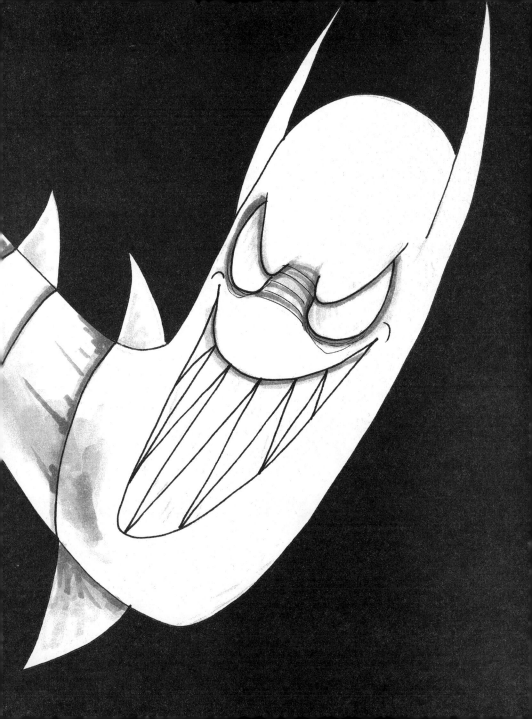

He needs our help . . .

Is it time . . . ?